For Matthias —B.M.

Copyright © 2003 by Michael Neugebauer Verlag,
an imprint of Nord-Süd Verlag AG, Gossau Zürich, Switzerland
First published in Switzerland under the title **Fritz Frosch.**
English translation copyright © 2003 by North-South Books Inc., New York

First published in the United States, Great Britain, Canada and Australia
in 2003 by North-South Books, an imprint of Nord-Süd Verlag AG, Gossau Zürich, Switzerland.

Distributed in the United States by North-South Books Inc., New York.

Library of Congress Cataloging-in-Publication Data is available.
A CIP catalogue record for this book is available from The British Library.
ISBN 0-7358-1847-9 (trade edition) 10 9 8 7 6 5 4 3 2 1
Printed in Italy

For more information about our books, and the authors and artists
who create them, visit our web site: www.northsouth.com

Farley Farts

Birte Müller

A MICHAEL NEUGEBAUER BOOK
NORTH-SOUTH BOOKS
NEW YORK/LONDON

For days, Farley the Frog had been having some rather noisy tummy trouble. He had to fart all the time. When he was eating, PFFFOOOTTT! When he was playing, PFFFOOOTTT! Even when he was sleeping, PFFFOOOTTT! It was really bothersome.

Otherwise, Farley was very content. He loved his life in the small village of Croakville and he had lots of friends.

His sister Frieda thought it was funny when Farley's farts made bubbles in the pond. It was like a Jacuzzi! But Mother Frog was worried. "He needs to go to the doctor," she declared.

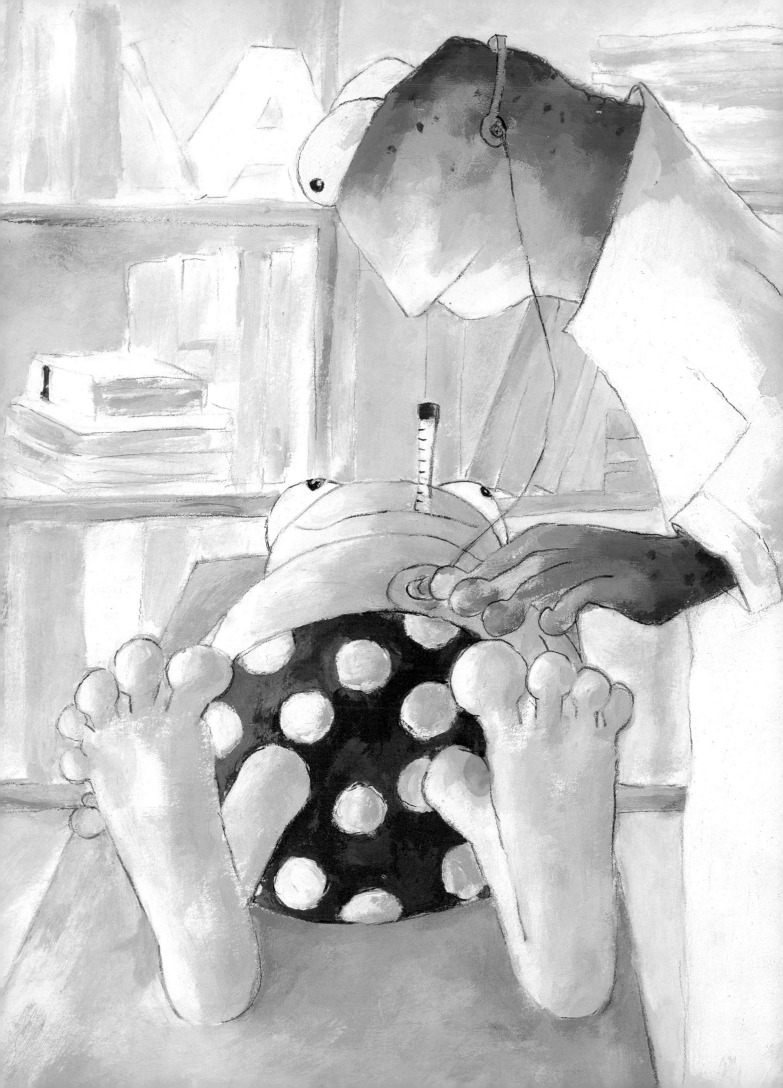

The doctor examined Farley. "Say aaaahhh and stick out your tongue," he said.

But the only thing that came out of Farley was a very loud fart: PFFFOOOTTT!

The doctor rolled his eyes and sputtered. "Nothing serious," he said, covering his nose. "Just, um, a case of a little gas. It will pass."

Unfortunately, it KEPT passing.

Everywhere Farley went, farts followed him. When
he was getting dressed, when he was washing up, in school,
not one hour of the day passed without Farley farting.
"What is two plus two?" asked the teacher.
PFFFOOOTTT! went Farley loudly.

All his classmates giggled. Farley turned very pale—he was so embarrassed. The teacher turned pale, too, because he was so angry. "How rude!" he scolded. "You have to stop right now. I'm going to have to talk to your parents."

Farley tried, but he couldn't stop farting. PFFFOOOTTT!
PFFFOOOTTT! PFFFOOOTTT!
His parents felt sorry for him. "Really, Farley," said his
mother, just as Farley made a loud PFFFOOOTTT right
under Grandma's nose. "Why don't you go to bed now,
and see if you can stop."

Farley went to his room, and tried as hard as he could to stop. But the longer he went without farting, the more his tummy hurt. It began to swell, and soon his pyjamas didn't fit him anymore.

The next morning, Farley felt very odd. He wasn't hungry or thirsty. His stomach had grown so big that he could barely fit through the door.

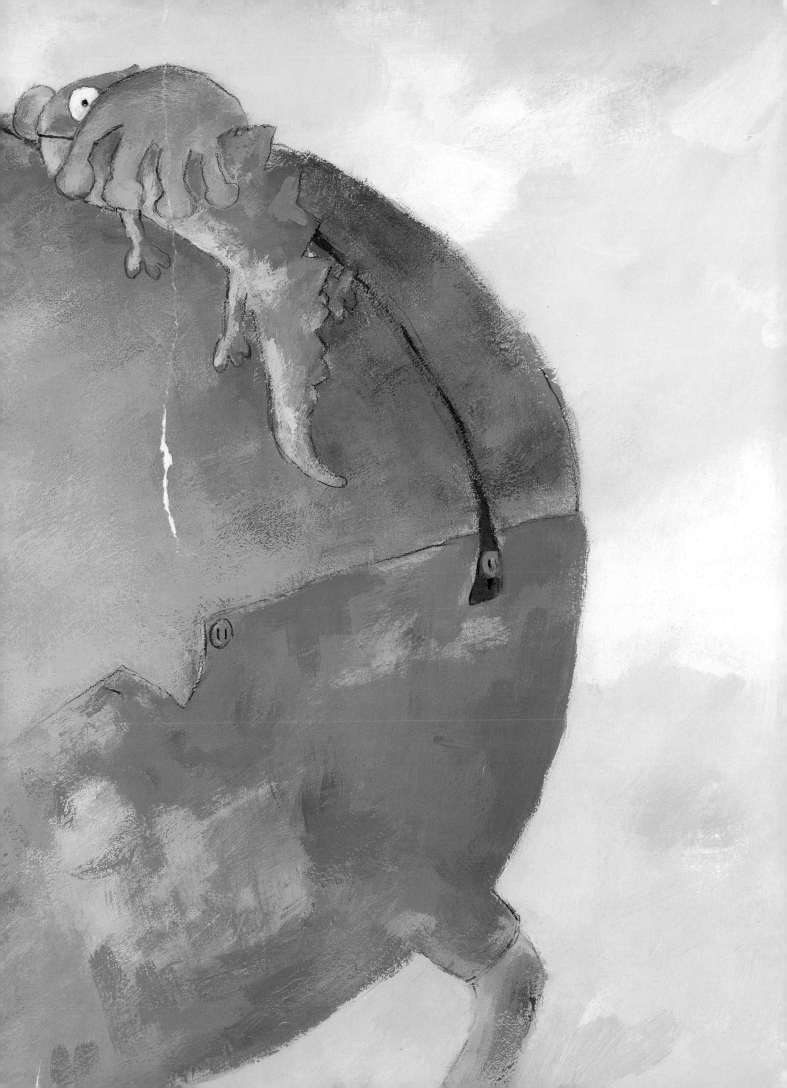

Outside, a tiny breeze lifted Farley like a hot-air balloon. There was nothing he could do. He sailed off into the sky. "Farley! Come back!" shouted Frieda, but Farley drifted higher and higher.

From way up high, the world below
looked so beautiful—the houses,
the fields, the hills on the horizon.
Farley was enjoying himself.
But down below his mother was crying
and his father was calling to him,
"Farley, please come back, please!"

"I can't," said Farley,
and drifted even higher.
Then Father Frog
had a brilliant idea.
"Fart, Farley, just
as loud as you can!"
But Farley couldn't hear him.
"What, Dad?"
"PFFFOOOTTT!" everyone shouted.

So Farley farted—one giant
PFFFFFFFOOOOOOOOOOOOOTTTTTTT!
And then Farley flipped and fluttered and floated
gently all the way down to the ground.

Farley lay flat on his back, looking
like an empty balloon.
Mother, Father, and Frieda rushed over.
Croaking happily, they hugged Farley.

That night, everyone ate Mother's speciality—bean soup. Later, the family snuggled together on the sofa.

Father Frog stroked Farley's belly gently.
Suddenly, PFFFOOOTTT!
Someone farted—
but this time it wasn't Farley!